This beautiful book belongs to

____

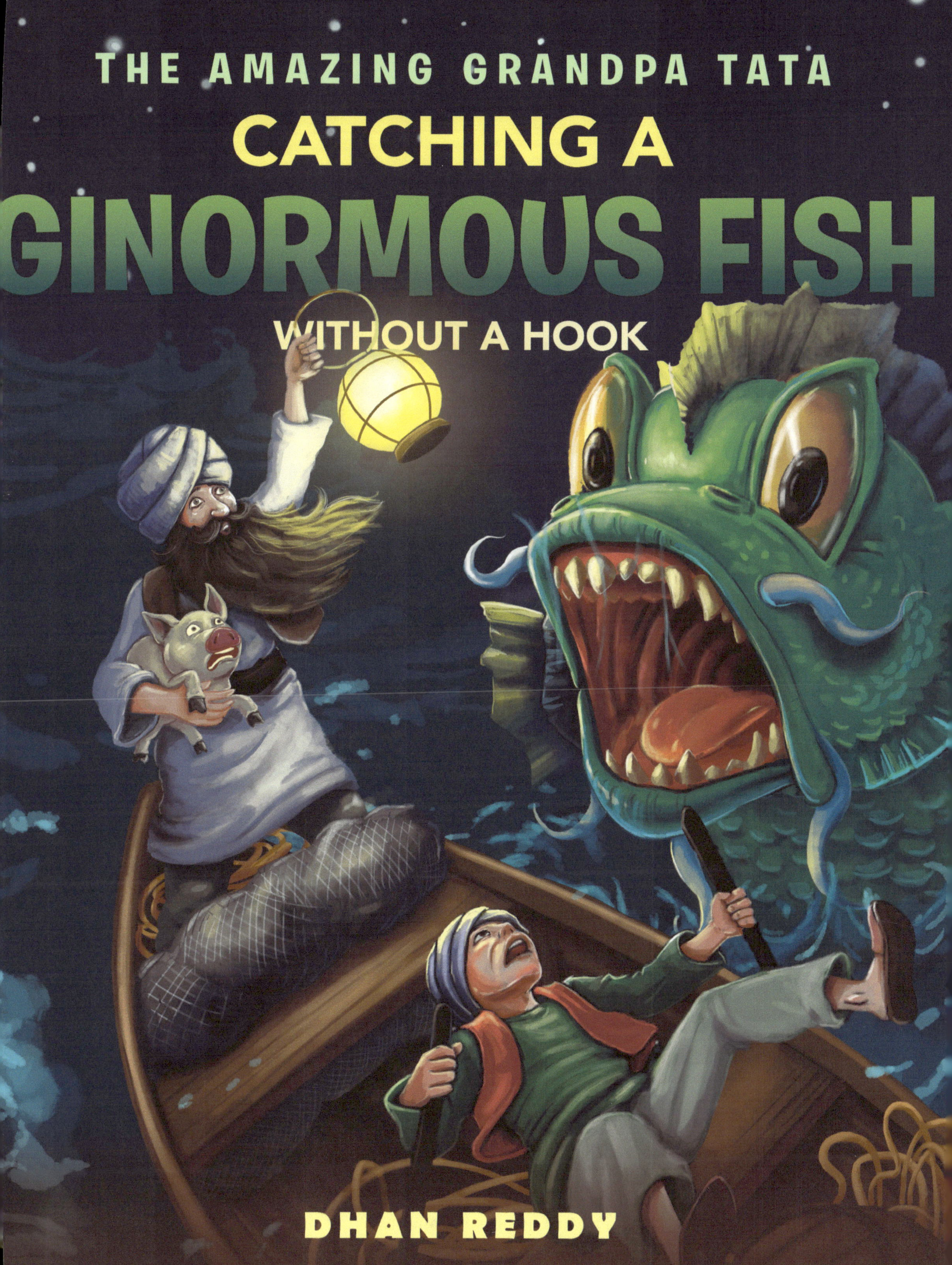

THE AMAZING GRANDPA TATA
CATCHING A
GINORMOUS FISH
WITHOUT A HOOK
DHAN REDDY

Printed in New York by:

OMNIBOOK CO.
99 Wall Street, Suite 118
New York, NY 10005
USA
+1 202-738-1322
www.omnibookcompany.com

First Edition

For e-book purchase: Kindle on Amazon, Barnes and Noble
Book purchase: Amazon.com, Barnes & Noble, and www.omnibookcompany.com
Omnibook titles may be purchased in bulk for educational, business, fund-raising, or sales promotional use.
For more information please e-mail info@omnibookcompany.com

Once upon a time...

Grandpa Tata lived in
a small village with his
son, daughter-in-law
and grandchildren
not far from the sea.

His favorite grandchild was Dinesh. Dinesh spent most of his time with his father hauling fish into the boat. He was quite an experienced little fisherman.

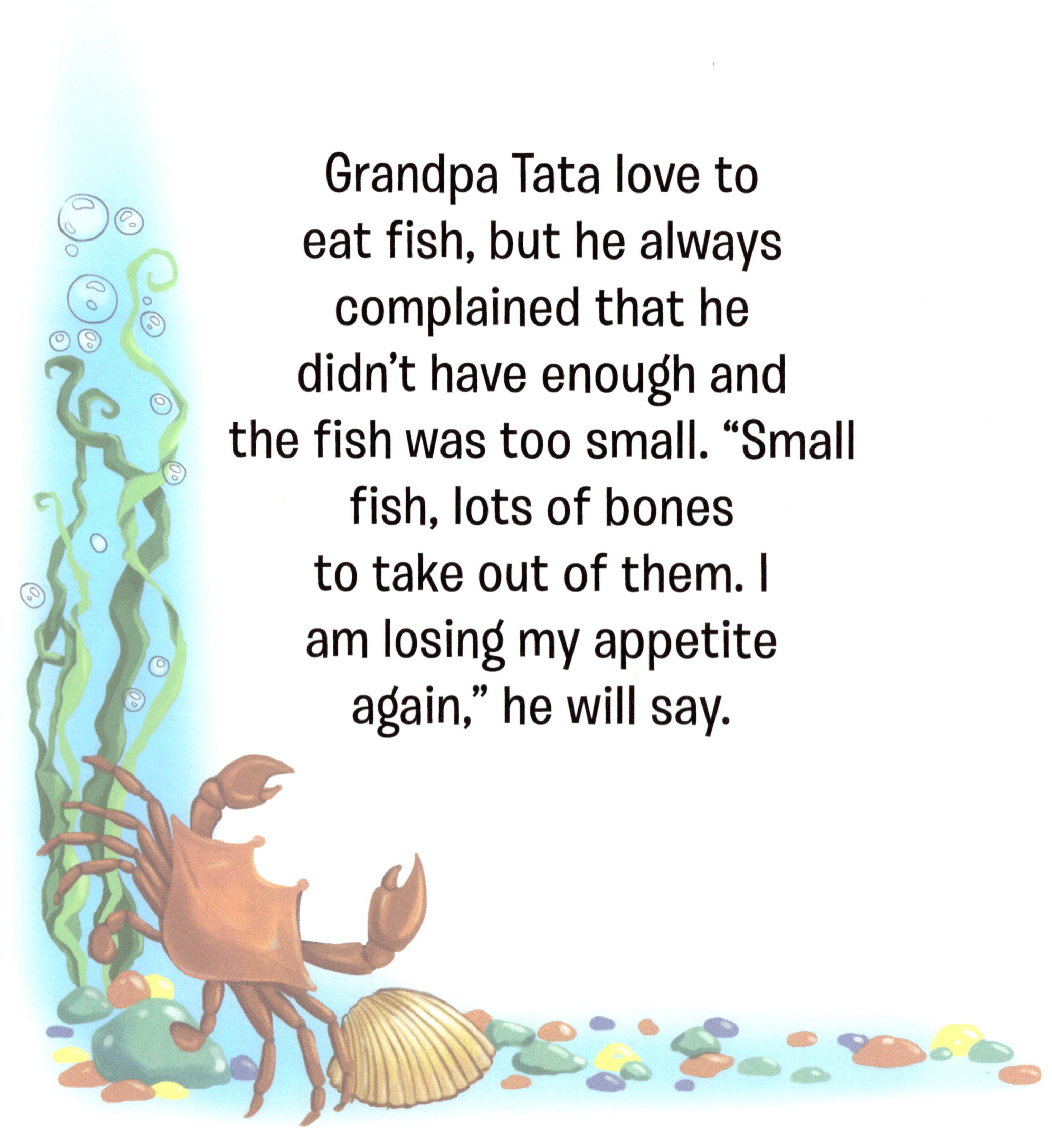

Grandpa Tata love to
eat fish, but he always
complained that he
didn't have enough and
the fish was too small. "Small
fish, lots of bones
to take out of them. I
am losing my appetite
again," he will say.

Every day, Dinesh and his father went to the sea to catch fish and every time they tried to catch a bigger fish.

When he got home,
Dinesh's mother
cooked the fish and
gave Grandpa Tata the
biggest piece of it .

Still he complained
that the fish was
too small.

Dinesh's father
thought, maybe his wife
didn't give his father a
big piece of fish.

So, one day Dinesh's
father hid in the dinner
area and he saw his wife
serve his father a big
piece of fish which he
had caught that day.

He came out of hiding, "Father, my wife had served you the best biggest piece fish which I just caught today. Father you still complained that it is a small piece. That is the biggest fish I caught so far."

"How big a fish you are
talking about?"

Angrily, he left Grandpa Tata alone. Dinesh tiptoed into Grandpa Tata's room and sat down on a cushion on the floor. He was a rapt listener and Grandpa's adventures and suggestions excited his interest.

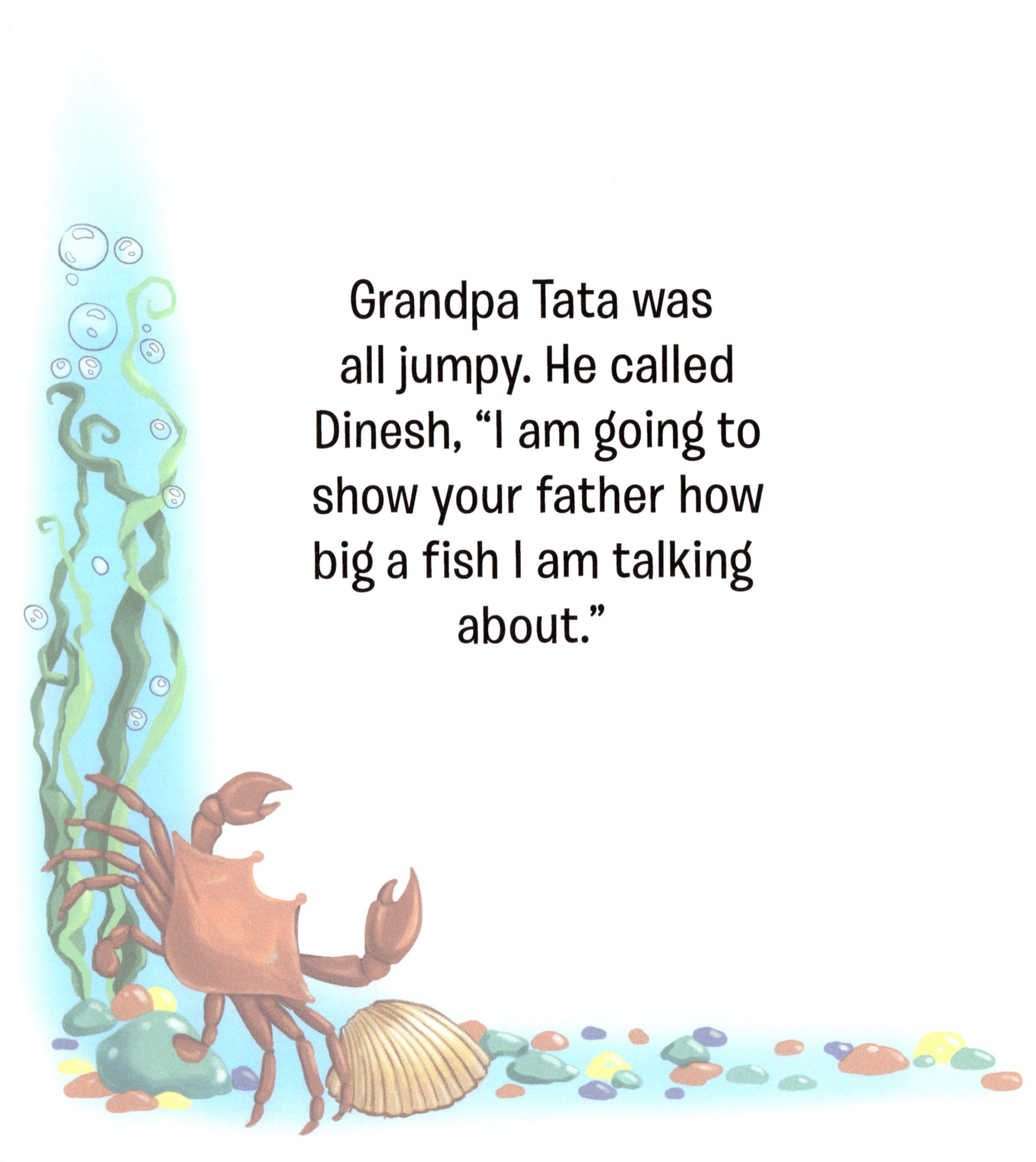

Grandpa Tata was all jumpy. He called Dinesh, "I am going to show your father how big a fish I am talking about."

Dinesh, you find a row
boat with oars, a piglet
and an oil lamp . Hide
the boat so that no one
knows about it. When it
is evening, and it starts
to get dark , we will go
to the sea to catch a big
fish."
The trip promised to be
long and adventurous.

Dinesh did just what Grandpa Tata told him to do. He got a boat with oars, an oil lamp and hid them near the sea. He found out where he could get the piglet the last moment.

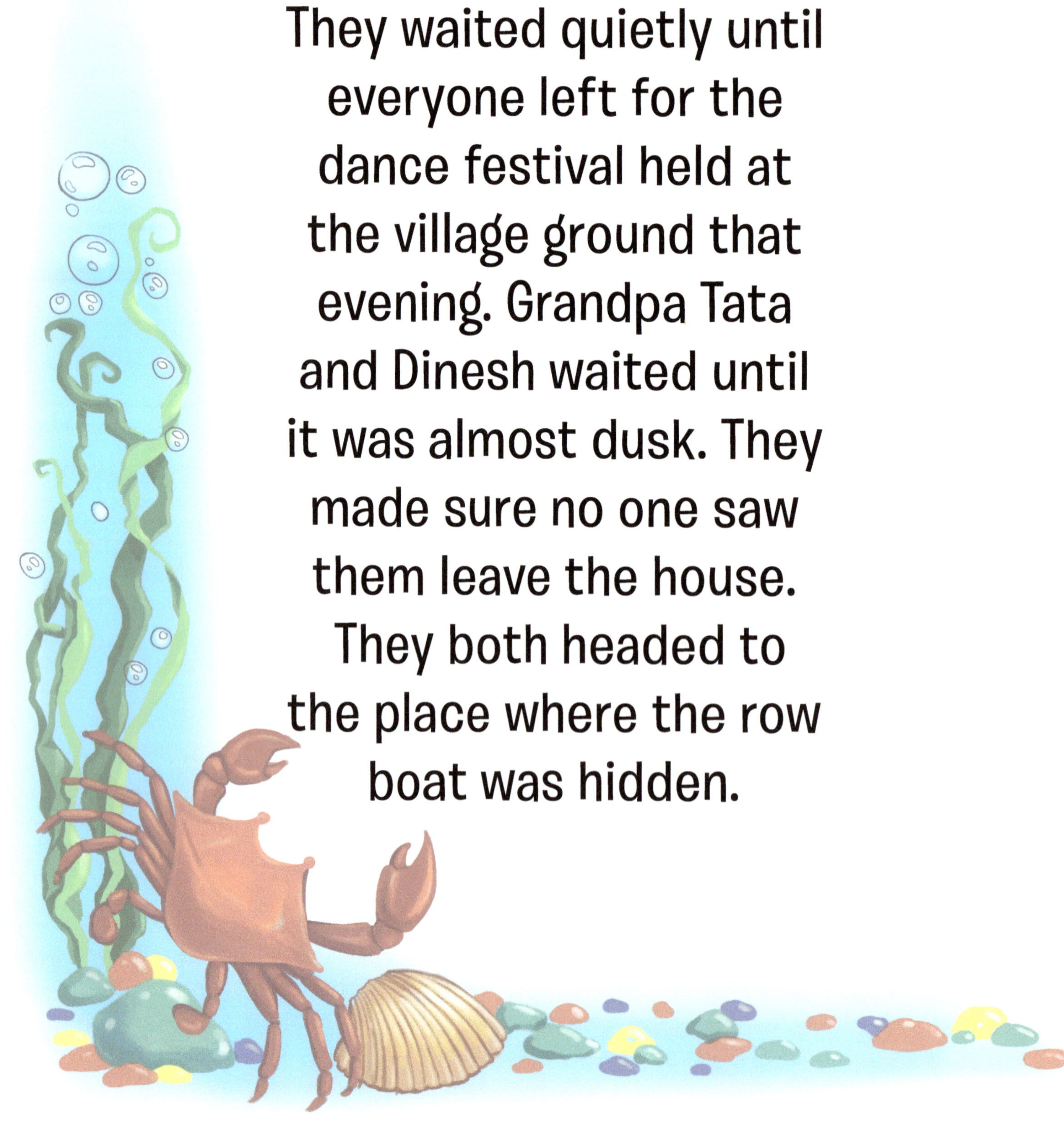

They waited quietly until everyone left for the dance festival held at the village ground that evening. Grandpa Tata and Dinesh waited until it was almost dusk. They made sure no one saw them leave the house. They both headed to the place where the row boat was hidden.

On the way, they grabbed the piglet from the sleeping mother pig. "We will bring piglet home soon," whispered Dinesh.

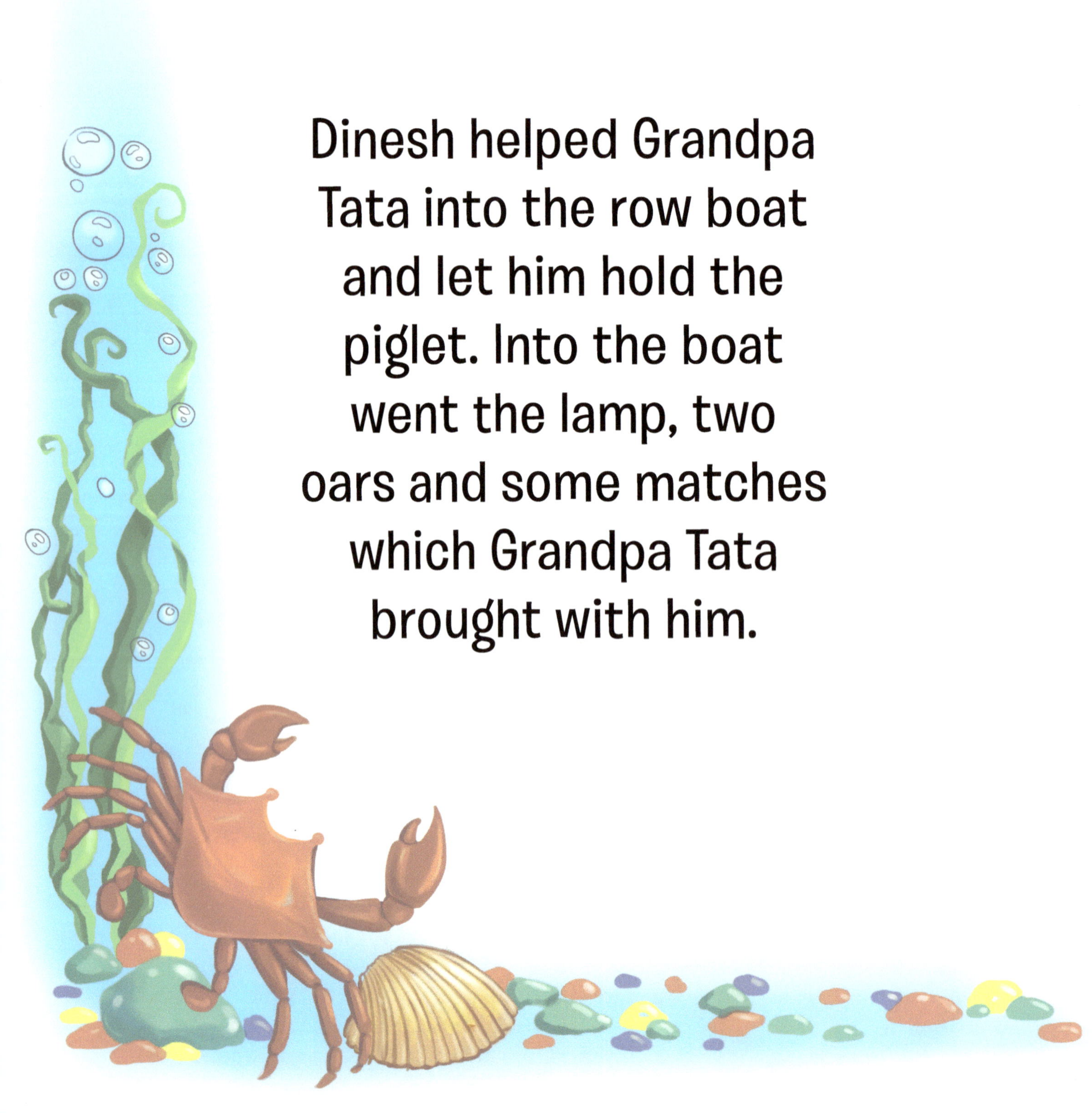

Dinesh helped Grandpa Tata into the row boat and let him hold the piglet. Into the boat went the lamp, two oars and some matches which Grandpa Tata brought with him.

Dinesh could feel the flow of sand cascade down his ankles as he pushed the boat right into the water and then climbed in. He started to row the boat into the deep water of the ocean.

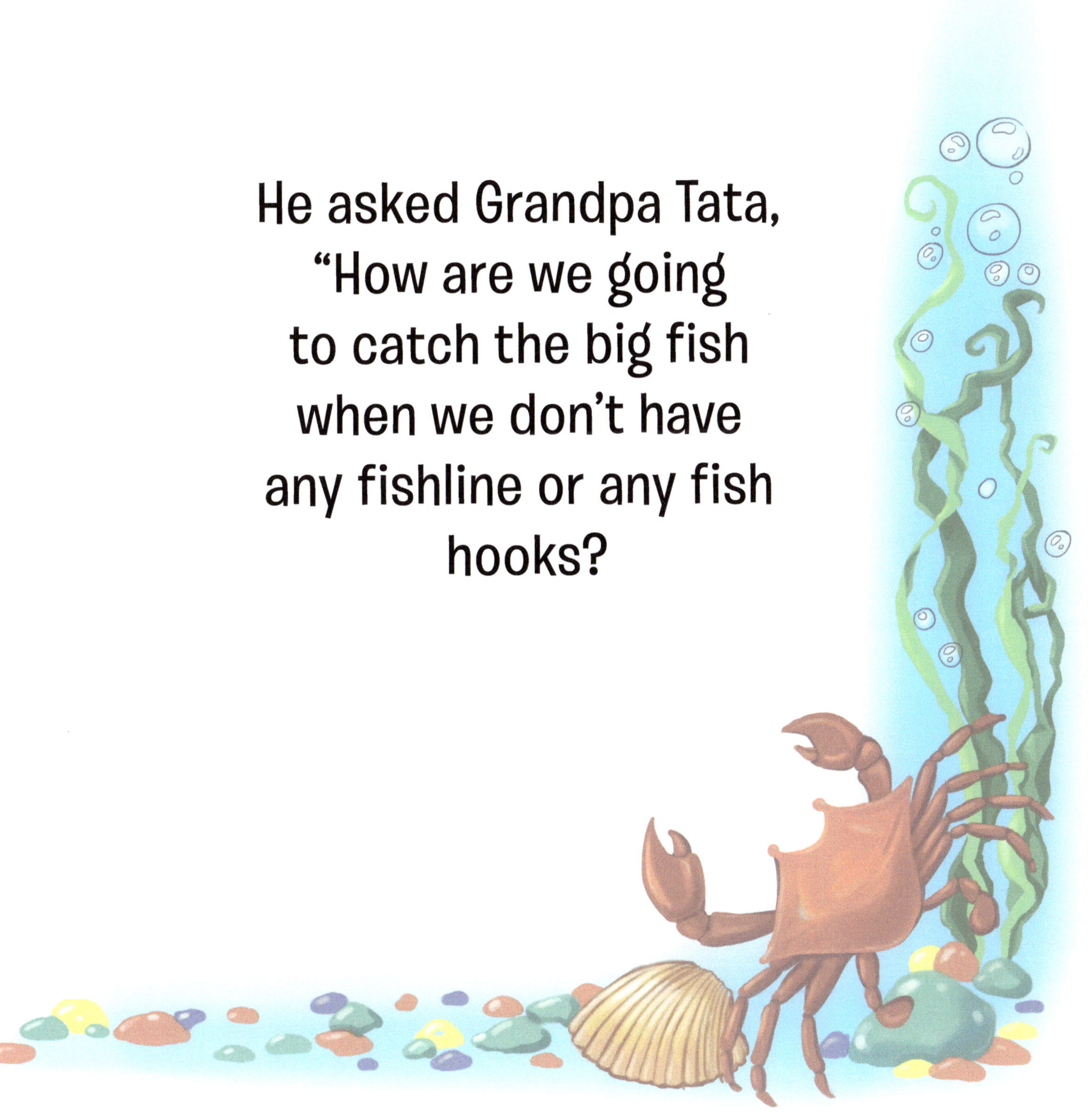

He asked Grandpa Tata, "How are we going to catch the big fish when we don't have any fishline or any fish hooks?

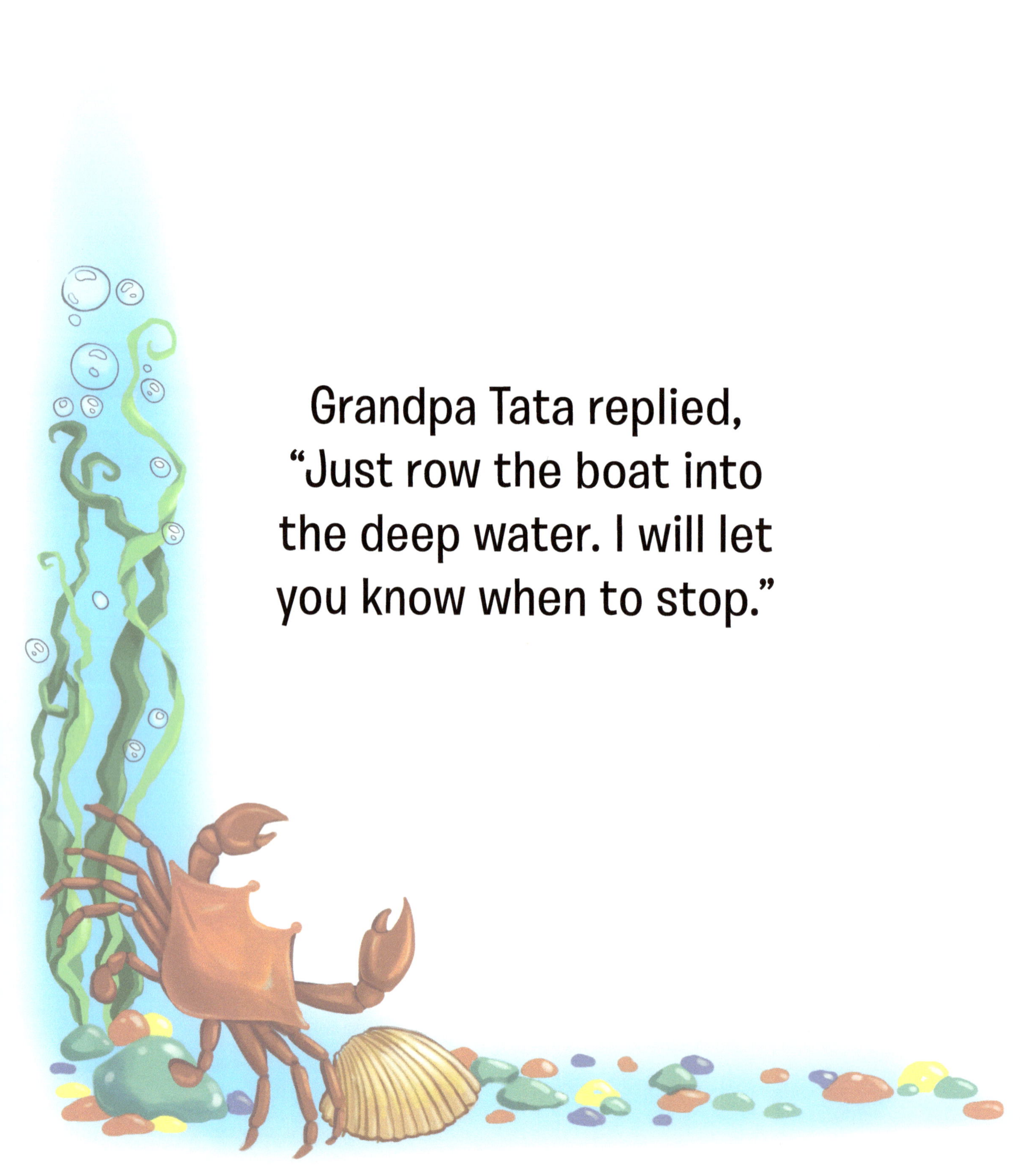

Grandpa Tata replied,
"Just row the boat into
the deep water. I will let
you know when to stop."

From the boat Dinesh
could see the shore
begin to disappear as he
rowed the boat into the
deeper water. Soon it
was completely out of
sight .

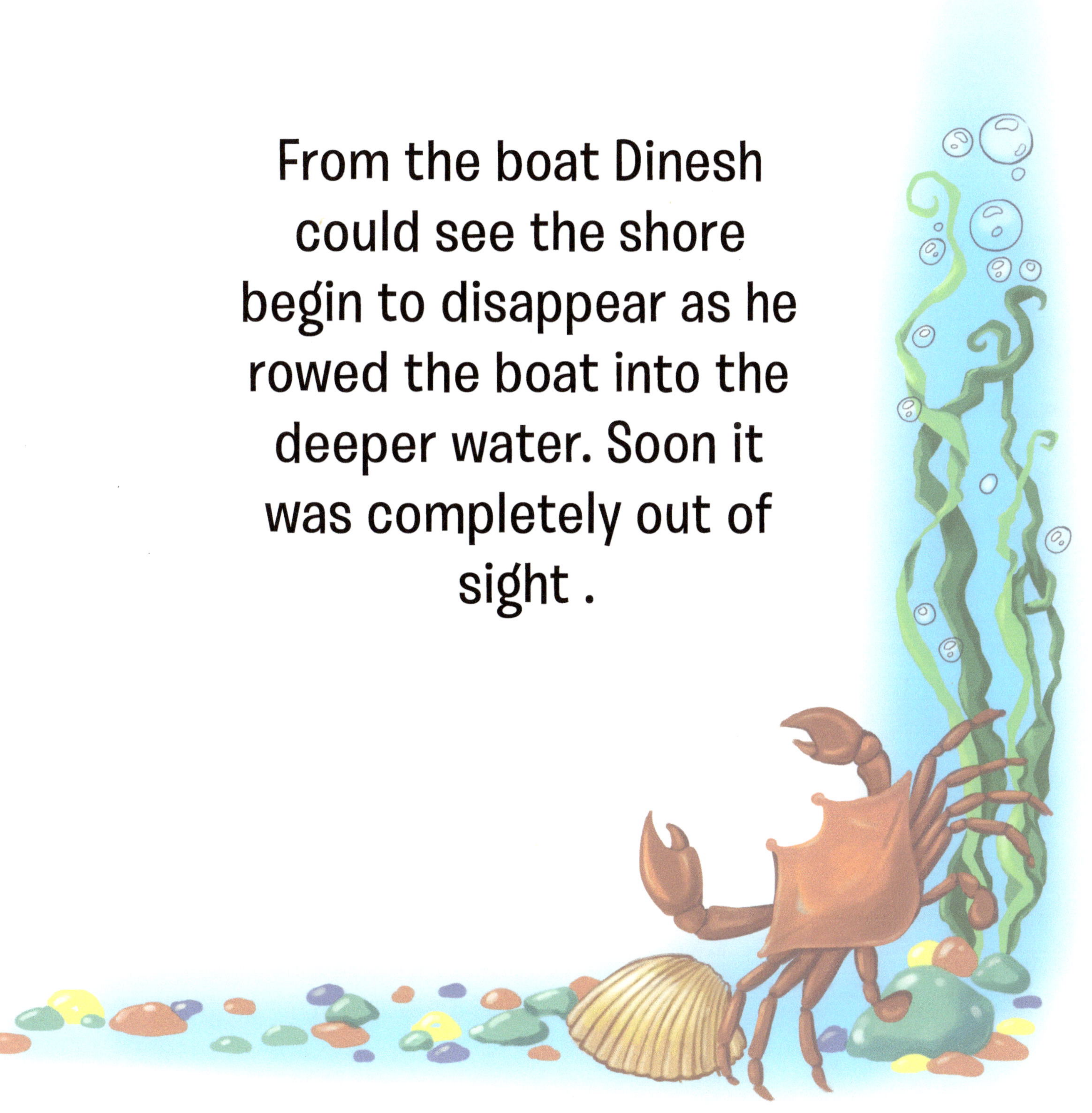

Finally, Grandpa Tata commanded Dinesh to stop rowing. It was quiet all around them.

He listened and then
he started to light the
oil lamp. Then he took
the piglet in his arm and
squeezed his neck.

The piglet squealed ear
piercing noises. Again he
squeezed the piglet's
neck and the piglet
let out more loud ear
piercing noises.

Now, there were some
wave movements in the
water and the boat
started to move from
side to side.

"Dinesh, could you see anything moving? I feel the movements in the water", said Grandpa Tata.

With an exclamation
of surprise Dinesh
answered, "Yes,
Grandpa, I see something
moving far away and
it seems to be coming
towards us."

Now, Grandpa Tata
lit the lamp higher and
brighter and lifted it way up.

As Grandpa Tata held
the lamp high, the
gigantic fish's eyes shone
big and bright.

"I see two big lights shining far away," called back Dinesh.

Grandpa Tata replied, "Then start rowing back. We are going back home now. The rapid movements made by the big fish will help push the boat faster towards the shore."

Grandpa Tata held
the lamp high with one
hand. With the piglet
placed between his
legs, he squeezed the
piglet's neck. The
piglet again squealed
ear piercing noises.

Dinesh rowed the boat with all his strength. The big waves made by the big fish were pushing the boat faster towards the shore.

Grandpa Tata kept on squeezing the piglet's neck. The squealing noises of the piglet made the big fish move more faster and quicker towards the boat.

In no time the boat was
thrown on the shore
and the big fish started
to look more like a
ginormous fish with
huge glowing eyes.

It was making lots of
loud screaming noises.

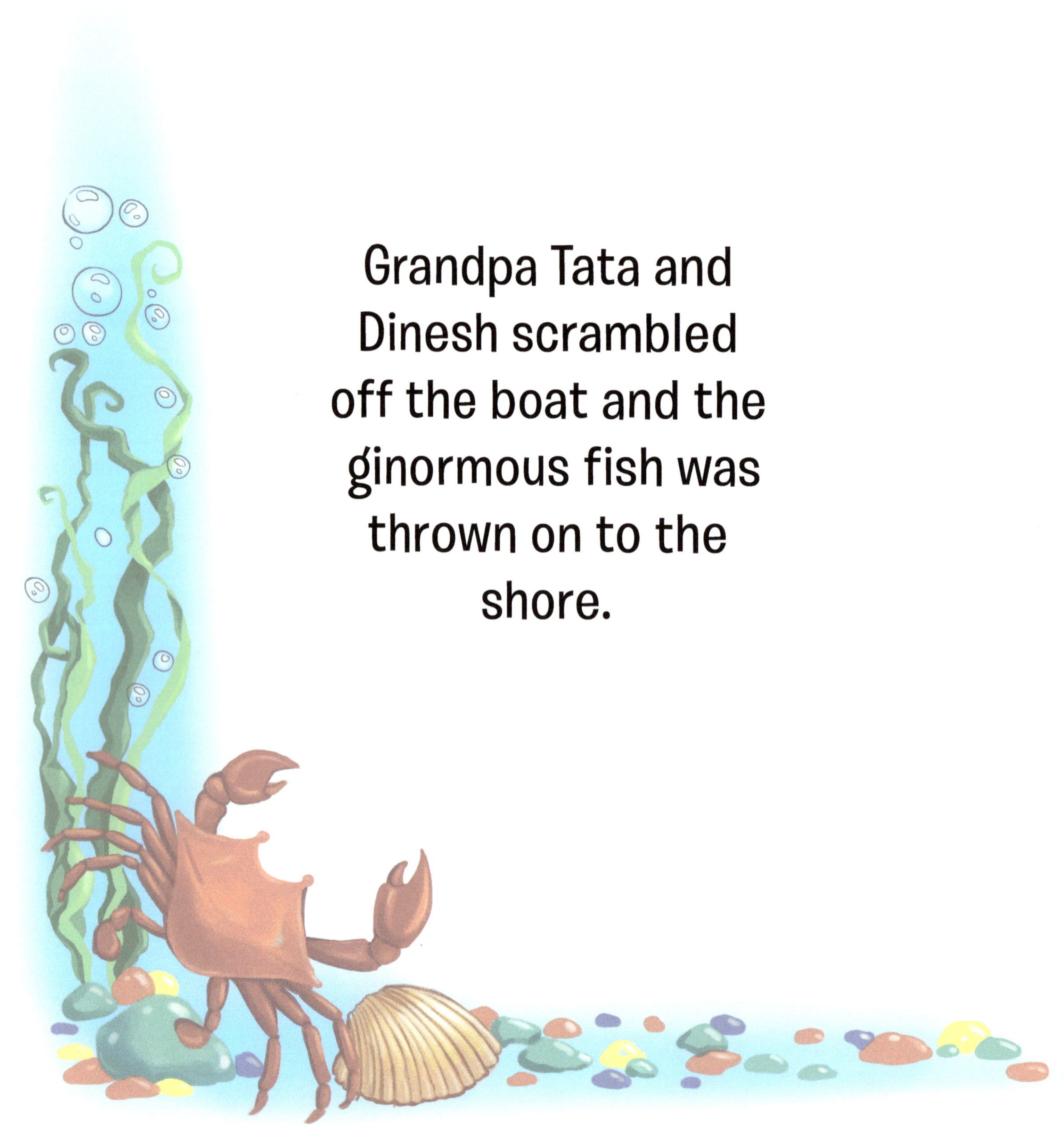

Grandpa Tata and
Dinesh scrambled
off the boat and the
ginormous fish was
thrown on to the
shore.

All the village people ran over to see what was happening. So too, Dinesh's father and mother with the kids followed the crowds.

There was quite a lot
of excitement now.

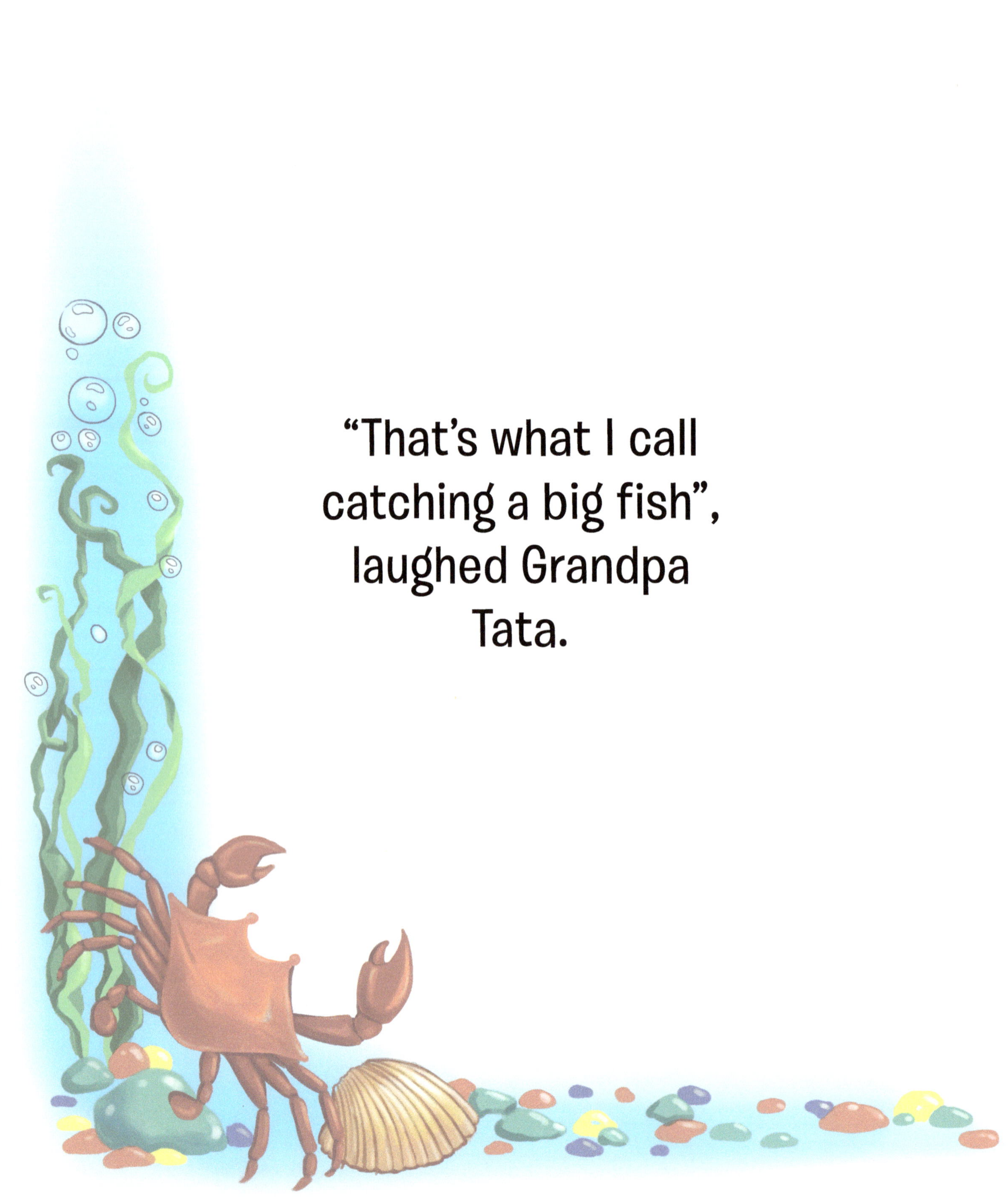

"That's what I call catching a big fish", laughed Grandpa Tata.

Soon, everyone
had a piece of the
Ginormous fish.

Dinesh's mother
served Grandpa Tata
the biggest piece of
the fish which she
cooked in her biggest
cooking pot.

The End